One-Minute Christmas Stories

One-Minute Christmas Stories

Adapted by

Shari Lewis

Author of
One Minute Bedtime Stories

Illustrated by Jan Palmer

Doubleday

NEW YORK • LONDON • TORONTO • SYDNEY • AUCKLAND

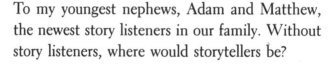

To my youngest nephews, Adam and Matthew,
the newest story listeners in our family. Without
story listeners, where would storytellers be?

Published by Doubleday, a division of Bantam Doubleday Dell Publishing Group, Inc., 666 Fifth Avenue, New York, New York 10103.

Doubleday and the portrayal of an anchor with a dolphin are trade-
marks of Doubleday, a division of Bantam Doubleday Dell Publishing
Group, Inc.

Library of Congress Cataloging-in-Publication Data

Lewis, Shari.
  One-minute Christmas stories.

  Summary: Stories for Christmas, some old, some new,
all in a format for reading in one minute.
  1. Christmas stories.   2. Children's stories.
[1. Christmas—Fiction.   2. Short stories] I. Title.
PZ5.L60p 1987   [Fic]   86-29146
ISBN 0-385-23424-4

Contents

To the Parents

As soon as the turkey has made its personal sacrifice for the national good, one burning question arises on the lips of children throughout the nation: "How many days till Christmas?"

Now, this is one of the two questions which children use to drive their parents crazy. (The other, uttered as soon as the car door slams shut, is "Are we almost there?")

These questions are apparently rituals of childhood.

Obviously, I can't do much about question no. 2. I mean, a car trip takes as long as a car trip takes.

But as *my* contribution to the national good, I've put together this book of one-minute Christmas stories in the hopes that you can fight ritual with ritual.

Let your youngsters know that no matter what else you read together, they will hear a one-minute Christmas story each night, and when the book is done, the enchanted evening will be near at hand.

Actually, storytelling already is a time-honored tradition at Christmas, with at least one real advantage over our contemporary, more commercial holiday habits: it doesn't cost anything.

Since religious intensity and preference vary from family to family, I have not concentrated on religious tales. Rather, I've looked for legends and fables that feature the magic of the holiday season and the reverence for kindness that is so comforting at Christmas.

Someone said, "The destiny of the world is determined less by the battles that are lost and won than by the stories it loves and believes in."*

I think the gentleness inherent in these Christmas stories adds a little extra warmth to cold winter days.

At heart we are all storytellers and story listeners, and Christmas is a lovely time to renew the tradition.

Shari Lewis

---

* That someone is Harold Goddard, "The Meaning of Shakespeare," Vol. II (University of Chicago Press).

Is There a Santa Claus?

A long time ago, a little girl named Virginia O'Hanlon wrote a letter to a newspaper. She said that some of her friends had told her there wasn't any Santa Claus, and she wanted to know if they were right or not.

The editor wrote, "Yes, Virginia, there *is* a Santa Claus. He exists as certainly as love and generosity exist, and you know that *they* give your life its highest beauty and joy.

"Your little friends are wrong, Virginia. How sad would the world be if there were no Santa Claus! It would be as sad as if there were no Virginias.

"Not believe in Santa Claus? You might as well not believe in fairies! Nobody *sees* Santa Claus, but that is no sign that there is no Santa Claus. The most real things in the world are those that neither children nor men can see. No Santa Claus! Thank God he lives, Virginia.

"And ten thousand years from now, he will still live and make glad the heart of childhood."

Capturing the Wild Turkey

Since his father had died, Philip and his mother had very little, and one of the many things they couldn't afford was a turkey for Christmas dinner. But in one of his books, Philip saw a full-color picture of the wild turkey of North America. Since they lived in North America, the little boy decided to catch a wild turkey for dinner.

So Philip went into the narrow space between his house and the next, and banged away at a wooden box with a hatchet

and some nails, until the nice painter who lived next door said, "What's all that noise about, Philip?"

Philip explained that he was going to trap a wild turkey of North America right there in the alley. He even showed his neighbor the picture in the book. The painter wished him luck.

Early the next morning, Philip and his mother went outside to check on the trap. There, flapping around in the box was a huge turkey.

"Look at the colors, Mother!" exclaimed Philip. "This must be the wild turkey of North America."

And sure enough, the turkey had gold feet, one bright green wing and a pink one, a yellow tail, and two red legs, neatly tied together. Philip's mother smiled at the neighbor's house, and she never asked why that turkey smelled so strongly of paint.

La Befana

Late one night somebody banged on the door of La Befana's cottage. "It's late! Go away!" she called, but the visitor banged again. She opened the door a crack. There was a tall bearded man: two more men behind him were seated on camels. Now the old woman was scared, because camels were very rare in Italy in those days. (Actually, they still are.)

"What do you want?" she asked.

"Madam," said the tall man, "we are three kings following a star to Bethlehem, but we've lost our way."

"Why do you want to go there?" said La Befana.

"We are bringing gifts for the newborn baby Jesus, the Son of God," said the man.

"Well," responded La Befana, "you'll have to ask someone else." She slammed the door, and the three visitors rode away.

But the woman couldn't forget what they had said, and the next morning she loaded her donkey with presents and went out to look for the Son of God.

Every year since then La Befana has gone from house to house in Italy, leaving gifts for the good children who live there, in hopes that one of them just might be the baby Jesus.

The Hollow Tree Inn

Coon, Possum, and Crow lived at the Hollow Tree Inn. Their neighbor, Mr. Dog, visited often and told them what went on in the Human's house, where *he* lived.

Once, Mr. Dog told how Santa Claus left Christmas presents in the children's stockings. Crow, Coon, and Possum had never heard of Santa Claus. They got excited and decided to hang their stockings, so Santa could bring *them* presents, too.

Now Mr. Dog knew that Santa only went to the Human's house, but he didn't say anything. Next day, he took all the money he'd been saving and bought a lot of presents, then went to the Human's attic and found a Santa suit. It didn't really fit him, but he wore it anyway.

14

Christmas Eve, Mr. Dog sneaked into the Hollow Tree Inn and filled the three stockings hanging there. Then Mr. Dog sat down in the rocking chair to rest for a minute and admire his handiwork.

Next morning, Coon, Crow, and Possum were thrilled to find that Santa had not only paid them a visit and stuffed their stockings, but Santa was still there, asleep in the chair!

Mr. Dog woke up, took off his beard, and laughed, and they all agreed that the first Christmas at Hollow Tree Inn had been a great success.

Little Wolff and His Wooden Shoes

A poor boy named Little Wolff wore ragged clothes, but was grateful to have a good pair of wooden shoes to keep his feet warm and dry.

The richer children in his school laughed at Little Wolff because his clothing looked so different from theirs.

Now, in Holland, Santa Claus fills *shoes* instead of stockings. And on this particular Christmas Eve, all the students in Little Wolff's class were hurrying home to place their wooden

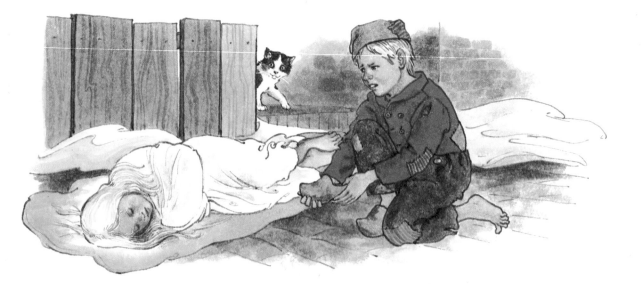

shoes by the fireplace when they passed a small child asleep on the street. The little one had no shoes on her feet.

Little Wolff's classmates didn't stop, but they did sneer and call the child nasty names. Not Little Wolff: he looked at the child's bare feet and thought "If this child has no shoes, where will Santa leave his presents?"

As poor as he was, Little Wolff took off one of his own wooden shoes, and gave it to this child who had none.

That night, before Little Wolff went to bed, he laid his one remaining shoe by the fireplace.

When he awakened, the boy's entire room was filled with wonderful presents. You see, the barefoot child on the street had been an angel, and Little Wolff was rewarded for his kindness.

As for the other students, when they awoke, the only thing in *their* shoes was mud!

Christmas on the Prairie

Cowboy John lived alone. One wintery day, he set out with his rifle to hunt up a few prairie chickens, or perhaps a buffalo, for Christmas dinner. After a while, the sky got dark, the wind blew up, and he was caught in the midst of the worst blizzard he'd ever seen.

Suddenly, through the swirling snow, John found himself staring at the hairy face of a big bull buffalo. John shot that buffalo, skinned the animal, and wrapped the skin around himself, to keep warm.

The storm let up as quickly as it had started, and John was startled to see that he was surrounded by wolves, looking for a meal. He tried to move, but discovered that the fresh buffalo skin wrapped around him had frozen solid and now held him tight.

He worked his right hand free and grabbed one of those wolves by the tail. The frightened wolf ran away and pulled the cowboy right along with him.

18

John bounced over the frozen prairie as though he were a fur sled. After a while, the skin thawed out, and then John let the wolf go. He jumped up, and, do you know, he found that he was only twenty feet from camp.

That Christmas dinner, John ate nothing but cornbread, but as he told himself over and over again, he was darned lucky to be alive.

Christmases are a lot tamer these days, aren't they?

Behind the White Brick

"Don't read when there's work to be done!" said Aunt Hetty. She seized the book from Jemima and threw it into the fireplace, where it went up in smoke. Jemima sat down and cried, for that book was her favorite. It was all about a girl named Flora, who lived in a lovely room.

Wondering if Flora had disappeared with the smoke, Jemima peered up the chimney, and there she saw a white brick among all the sooty ones.

"How could a brick stay white up there?" thought Jemima.

Suddenly Jemima felt herself to be floating up the chimney like a piece of dust. She stopped right in front of the white brick. That brick slid open, and to her astonishment Jemima saw Flora, her friend from the book. Flora was sitting in her room, just as it had been described in the first chapter.

Flora led Jemima to the next room, where lots of tiny men and women were making toys for Santa Claus. The two girls played with the toys until Jemima fell asleep.

When she awakened, she was sitting by the fireplace and Aunt Hetty was kissing her and saying she was sorry. Hetty gave Jemima a *new* storybook.

But for the rest of her days, whenever she lit a fire in that fireplace, Jemima thought of the Christmas day she had spent with her once-in-a-storybook friend, Flora.

The Night It Rained Toys

One Christmas Eve it rained toys. This is how it happened:

In the year 1910 Santa Claus caught a cold. Not an ordinary cold, but a whopper! His nose got so red that the elves started calling him Rudolph. Clearly, he was too sick to make his usual trip around the world.

Santa *wanted* to go, of course, for without him who would deliver the toys? But Mrs. Claus was firm. Santa must stay in bed!

"But the children—!" he protested.

Mrs. Claus grinned and volunteered: "I'll drive the sled," she said.

Santa started ho-ho-ho'ing. "No one can drive that old sleigh but me," he insisted, and then he sneezed and sneezed some more.

It was decided. Mrs. Claus would deliver the toys.

Santa instructed the reindeer not to go too fast, and with that off they flew.

The sleigh was sailing along and everything was going well when Mrs. Claus saw a great light in the sky. It was swirling right at her. The light, that night in 1910, was Halley's Comet.

To avoid being hit, Mrs. Claus swerved the sled, and for a moment it tipped over onto its side. The sturdy old sleigh quickly righted itself and no one was hurt, but all the toys in the sack fell out, and they poured down onto the town directly below.

22

And in that little village, everyone remembers Christmas Eve 1910, as "The Night It Rained Toys."

When Mrs. Claus arrived back at the North Pole (to get another load of presents), Santa just laughed and said, "Better to give away extra toys, than no toys at all!"

Mrs. Brownlow's Christmas Party

Mrs. Brownlow decided to give a party for the children of all her *nice* friends. She hand-wrote thirty invitations and gave them to her son Bob to deliver personally.

All Christmas Day the three Brownlows bustled about, getting ready for their guests, who were to arrive at five. At a quarter of five, Mr. Brownlow lit the candles on the tree. Through the window he saw a few ragged children in the street watching with interest as the food was laid on the table.

Soon there was a crowd outside of obviously hungry kids, the bigger ones holding up babies so they could get a better look.

Five o'clock passed. Not *one* of the guests arrived.

"Well," said Mr. Brownlow, embarrassed, "seein' as the

well-off folks haven't accepted our invitation, don't you think we better invite some of the others in?"

The room filled with poor children from the street.

They had a wonderful time. After the ice cream was served, young Bob sat down for the first time and felt a bulge in his pocket. He reached in and pulled out the invitations: he'd forgotten to deliver them!

"I'm glad you did," said Mrs. Brownlow. "This was the best Christmas party one could ask for."

The Mouse Who Didn't Believe in Santa Claus

Squeaknibble was a mouse who didn't believe in anything she hadn't seen, and she'd never seen a cat.

"You're just trying to scare me," she told her parents. "There are no cats."

Christmas Eve, Squeaknibble's mother put her to bed early so that Santa Claus could leave his presents while she was asleep. After the lights were out, Squeaknibble thought, "I don't believe there *is* a Santa Claus. *I've* never seen him."

She left her bed and the safety of the family mouse hole to turn cartwheels on the living room rug.

Suddenly, a large shadowy figure loomed like a monster ghost all covered in white fur. The creature purred, "Don't be afraid, little mousie, it's only me, Santa Claus, come to bring you a present of delicious cheese."

"Oh," said Squeaknibble, "how nice."

Christmas came and Christmas went, and little Squeaknibble was never seen again. And when the real Santa Claus came to the mouse hole, he reminded the other mice that nothing good has *ever* come of not believing in Santa Claus.

The Christmas Rose

One cold day, Wilhelm took his ax and a bit of bread and wandered into the woods to find a Christmas tree for his sister Griselda. "I may not have money for presents," he thought, "but a fine fir tree would brighten the cabin." As he trudged through the snow, he came upon a rabbit caught in a trap. He

freed it, and the rabbit hopped away, calling, "Thank you, and happy Christmas!"

Deeper in the woods, Wilhelm found a mouse, almost dead from hunger. He fed it a few crumbs of bread. The mouse perked up and ran off, squeaking, "Merry Christmas, Wilhelm, and thank you so much."

In the darkest part of the forest, where no one had been before, Wilhelm found a wonderful green bush with a single red rose on the very top.

Wilhelm plucked the rose for Griselda and ran home. But no sooner had he gotten inside than the King knocked on the door.

"Congratulations, Wilhelm," said the King. "You found the magic Christmas rose that no one has ever seen before. Give me a small piece to plant in my garden, and I'll give you a sack of gold."

With the King's gold, Wilhelm and his sister Griselda had the best Christmas ever. So if you find a rose in the snow, deep in the woods, pick it. Who knows, it might be the magic Christmas rose!

The Horse Who Thought He Was a Reindeer

On a farm near a river lived a horse named Mack. His job was to pull the farmer's wagon back and forth over an old wooden bridge—hard work, but Mack never seemed to mind.

Now, ever since he was a colt, Mack had always loved Christmas. His red wagon, decked with holly, would be loaded with presents and happy people. But most of all, Mack loved the stories he would hear about Santa Claus's reindeer. Whenever a load was too heavy, Mack would pretend that he, too, could fly. This seemed to make his job easier.

One Christmas Eve, smack in the middle of a big storm, the farmer's little son took sick. The worried parents loaded the boy into Mack's wagon and they raced toward town. The wind blew, and the snow piled higher and higher until the old wooden bridge collapsed.

But because of the swirling snow, the people in the wagon couldn't see, and they kept heading straight for that bridge that was no longer there.

Too late to stop, Mack saw that the bridge had fallen, and he prayed, "If there is a Santa Claus, and he does have reindeer, let *me* be one, just this once!"

Suddenly, Mack realized that he was no longer running on the ground. He was soaring over the icy river. When he landed on the distant bank, he galloped straight to the doctor's house, and the little boy was saved.

Mack never bothered pretending to fly again—but he would never forget the night when he had really done it!

The Glastonbury Thorn

There once was a man named Joseph of Arimathea. Joseph was very tired, for no matter how hard he tried, he couldn't fall asleep. Every time he would close his eyes, a vision of an angel would appear before him. The angel kept saying, "Go to England and establish the church there. Go to England. Go to England."

After many nights of this, Joseph decided to go to England.

As a walking stick to help him on his long trip, Joseph chose a thorn staff, in honor of the plant that once shielded Jesus.

When Joseph arrived in England, he found that the King

didn't want a church. Definitely not. Not of *any* kind. Not at all.

Joseph took the King to the city of Glastonbury. (That's where Joseph wished to build this church.) Still the King absolutely refused. Joseph was so angry and frustrated, he threw his staff of thorns into the ground. Instantly it bloomed! Everyone was amazed.

The King, knowing a miracle when he saw one, was really impressed. He finally agreed to build the church in Glastonbury, and the King became the church's first convert.

And at long last, Joseph of Arimethea was able to get some sleep.

The Shoemaker and the Elves

Three days before Christmas, a poor shoemaker realized that he had no money to buy leather with which to make even *one* more pair of shoes. All he could find around his shop were tiny mismatched scraps, out of which he couldn't make even one shoe, so he didn't try. Instead, he went to sleep.

However, by morning, *someone* had sewn those silly scraps into fancy footwear, indeed!

The shoemaker sold the fine finished shoes for lots of money, bought a *big* piece of leather, left it on his workbench, and once again went to bed.

But this time he *didn't* sleep. He watched, and at midnight he saw two tiny naked gnomes enter by the window, swiftly sew beautiful boots out of the leather, and then, just as swiftly, hop into the snow and disappear!

Next morning, when the shoemaker sold the beautiful boots, he got enough money for lots of leather, but with some of his earnings he bought bright bits of wool. All that day he sewed tiny clothes.

At midnight, when the little men came again to help the hardworking shoemaker, they found their warm gifts waiting for them under the Christmas tree.

Jumping for joy, they put on the clothes and hopped off into the snow, leaving behind two thank-you notes and, of course, one grateful shoemaker!

The Festival of the Lights

It was 1943. It was winter. It was wartime and food was scarce. Many Dutch Jews had been hunted down and sent away by the Nazi soldiers. That's what had happened to Isaac's parents, and it might have happened to him, but an old Christian couple had hidden Isaac away in their attic, though if the Nazis found out, it might mean their own deaths.

Now this couple loved Christmas and had saved tiny bits of candles and cans of food so they could celebrate their holiday with a small tree and a big meal.

They told Isaac about Christmas. He told them about Hanukkah, the Jewish celebration right before Christmastime,

when Jews light candles for each of the eight days of the festival. The more Isaac remembered, the more he missed his family and the sadder he became. The old couple saw Isaac suffering and suffered with him.

"Let's do what we can," they agreed.

And on the first day of Hanukkah, to Isaac's delight, there were two candles shining brightly in his attic, and for each day thereafter, the couple lit another candle and opened another can of food that they had been saving for their own holiday.

There would be no signs for Christmas for them this year, but their gift was the joy they saw reflected from the Hanukkah candles in Isaac's eyes.

The Gift of the Magi

Jim and Della were poor, but they had two things of which they were proud: one was Della's beautiful long hair, and the other was Jim's fine pocket watch (which had belonged to his father before him).

One Christmas, Della wanted to buy Jim a platinum chain for his watch. She didn't have enough money, so she cut off her beautiful hair and sold it to a wig maker for twenty dollars.

When Jim came home on Christmas Eve, he couldn't believe his eyes. He had loved Della's hair, and now it was so short, she looked like a boy.

"Don't be angry," said Della. "I needed the money to buy your Christmas present."

Jim hugged his wife and said, "Unwrap my gift for you, and you'll understand why I was so surprised."

Della tore open the package. Guess what Jim had gotten

her—a pair of very expensive tortoise-shell combs for the beautiful hair she no longer had.

Now it was Della's turn to give Jim his present, the gold watch chain to go with his father's watch. Jim looked at the chain and smiled. "Della, we'll have to put our Christmas gifts away for a while. You see, I sold my watch to get the money to buy those combs for your hair. Let's just put our Christmas supper up, and enjoy what we *do* still have, which is—each other."

And that's exactly what they did!

How Santa Claus Came to Simpson's Bar

One Christmas Eve a hundred years ago, in a tiny mining town called Simpson's Bar, a big miner named Dick Bullins met a sick little boy named Johnny, who had never even *heard* of Santa Claus. Bullins decided to give the child his first Christmas. Although the night was freezing, the big miner mounted his horse Jovita and headed for the distant village of Tuttleville to buy some toys.

They crossed Rattlesnake Creek and reached Tuttleville at two in the morning. Dick banged on the door of the store and got the owner out of bed. It was three A.M. before he was back on his horse with a bag full of toys.

Just before Rattlesnake Creek, a robber tried to shoot Dick off his horse, but Jovita reared up and knocked the man to the ground. Wounded, with a bullet in his arm, Dick managed to hang onto his horse, who galloped the rest of the way to Johnny's home.

The big miner stumbled off his horse and threw open the door.

"Put these toys in the boy's stocking," Dick said to Johnny's mother, "and tell him Santa Claus has come." Then Dick Bullins fainted.

The family nursed Dick back to health, and everyone knew that Santa Claus really *had* come to Simpson's Bar.

The Fir Tree

The Little Fir Tree wanted very much to be a grown-up tree and become the mast on a sailing ship, or at least an important telephone pole.

In the forest the sun shone brightly, birds sang, and sweet breezes whispered through his branches, but the Little Fir didn't enjoy it.

"I'm made for better things than this," he said.

Just before Christmas the small tree *was* cut down and taken to a fine house. Candles, colored glass balls, and silver icicles were attached to his limbs, and a tinsel star was placed at the very top. Presents were put at his feet.

"Oh," he thought, "this is terrific. What a life."

In the morning, the children sat under the tree and opened their presents.

Trembling with excitement, he waited all day and the next night for something else wonderful to happen, but in the morning, he was dragged out into the yard and thrown onto a pile of brush. The children, who had admired him just the night before, trampled his branches. The Little Fir thought, "If only I'd enjoyed the forest when I was able to. Now it's too late."

Then the man of the house set fire to the tree, and the Little Fir disappeared forever in a cloud of sweet-smelling smoke.

The Wrong Toy

On Christmas morning Billy woke up and limped downstairs to see what Santa had brought him. There, sitting under the tree, was a brand-new fire-engine red bicycle.

Obviously Santa had brought the wrong toy.

You see, ever since Billy had hurt his leg, he could barely walk. Now, he didn't really *want* to walk (he told himself), and riding a bike was out of the question!

But it *was* a good-looking bike. Billy sat on the shiny black seat. Too bad Santa gave me the wrong toy, he thought.

For days Billy just sat there on that bike.

One morning he muttered, "I certainly can't pedal it, but maybe I can coast."

He went outside and tried that, coasting back and forth, up and down the block, pushing against the sidewalk, first with one foot, then with both.

Billy was happy just to be outside again. After a week he was tired of coasting. He put his feet on the pedals. All that pushing had strengthened his legs a bit. He could tell.

"Maybe I can just pedal to the school yard," Billy whispered to himself. "Maybe this wasn't the wrong toy at all." Billy grinned. "By next Christmas," he said out loud, "all I'll need is a bell!"

And that's what he got!

A Visit from St. Nicholas

'Twas the night before Christmas, and all through the house
Not a creature was stirring, not even a mouse,

When out on the lawn there arose such a clatter,
I sprang from my bed to see what was the matter.

Away to the window I flew like a flash,
Tore open the shutters and threw up the sash.

And what to my wondering eyes should appear,
But a miniature sleigh and eight tiny reindeer,

With a little old driver, so lively and quick,
I knew in a moment it must be St. Nick.

As I drew in my head, and was turning around,
Down the chimney St. Nicholas came with a bound.

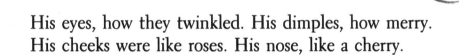

His eyes, how they twinkled. His dimples, how merry.
His cheeks were like roses. His nose, like a cherry.

He had a broad face and a little round belly,
That shook when he laughed like a bowl full of jelly.

He spoke not a word, but went straight to his work,
And filled all the stockings, then turned with a jerk,

And laying his finger aside of his nose,
And giving a nod, up the chimney he rose.

He sprang to his sleigh, to his team gave a whistle,
And away they all flew like the down of a thistle;

But I heard him exclaim, ere he drove out of sight,
"Happy Christmas to all, and to all a good night!"

About the Author

World-famous ventriloquist and puppeteer **Shari Lewis** (also known as Lamb Chop's mother) has been honored with five Emmy Awards, a Peabody, the Monte Carlo TV Award for World's Best Variety Show, and the 1983 Kennedy Center Award for Excellence and Creativity in the Arts. One of the few female symphony conductors, she has performed with and conducted more than one hundred symphony orchestras, including the National Symphony at the Kennedy Center, the Pittsburgh Symphony, the National Arts Centre Orchestra of Canada, and the Osaka National Symphony in Japan.

Besides the recently published *One-Minute Greek Myths*, Shari Lewis is the author of five previous books for Doubleday including *One-Minute Bible Stories—Old Testament, One-Minute Bible Stories—New Testament* (with Florence Henderson), *One-Minute Animal Stories, One-Minute Favorite Fairy Tales*, and *One-Minute Bedtime Stories. One-Minute Bedtime Stories* (available from Worldvision) and *One-Minute Bible Stories* (both Old and New Testament available from Magic Window/RCA/Columbia) are on home videocassettes. Shari Lewis is presently Chairman of the Board of Trustees of the International Reading Foundation and has served on the national board of the Girl Scouts of the U.S.A. A resident of Beverly Hills, California, Ms. Lewis is married to book publisher Jeremy Tarcher; their daughter, Mallory, is in the home video industry.

Jan Palmer has been illustrating children's books for almost twenty years. She currently lives in an old farmhouse which she is restoring in the Adirondacks in upstate New York.